MW01070001

MARVEL
SUPER HERO
SQUAD

MARVEL, Super Hero Squad, all characters, and the distinctive likenesses thereof are trademarks of Marvel Entertainment, LLC and its subsidiaries, and are used with permission. Copyright © 2010 Marvel Entertainment, LLC and its subsidiaries. Licensed by Marvel Characters B.V. www. marvel.com
All Rights Reserved.

Super Hero(es) is a co-owned registered trademark.

Except as permitted under the U.S. Copyright Act of 1976, no part of this publication may be reproduced, distributed, or transmitted in any form or by any means, or stored in a database or retrieval system, without the prior written permission of the publisher.

Little, Brown and Company • Hachette Book Group • 237 Park Avenue, New York, NY 10017
Visit our website at www.lb-kids.com • LB kids is an imprint of Little, Brown and Company.
The LB kids name and logo are trademarks of Hachette Book Group, Inc.

The publisher is not responsible for websites (or their content) that are not owned by the publisher.

First edition: September 2010 • 10 9 8 7 6 5 4 3 2

ISBN: 978-0-316-08486-4
CW
Printed in the United States of America

MARVEL
SUPER HERO SQUAD
THOR'S
BIG ADVENTURE
by Ray Santos
illustrations by Guido Guidi
LITTLE, BROWN & COMPANY
LB kids

Inside Super Hero Squad headquarters, an emergency call comes in for the Mighty Thor.

"What is it, my friend?" Thor asks the man on-screen.

"Thor, thy father, Odin, has requested thy hasty return," the helmeted man reports. "Asgard is under attack. The trickster Loki doth used his evil magic to make us thinketh that friends were at the gates . . . but when we opened them, it was Loki with an army of Sentinels."

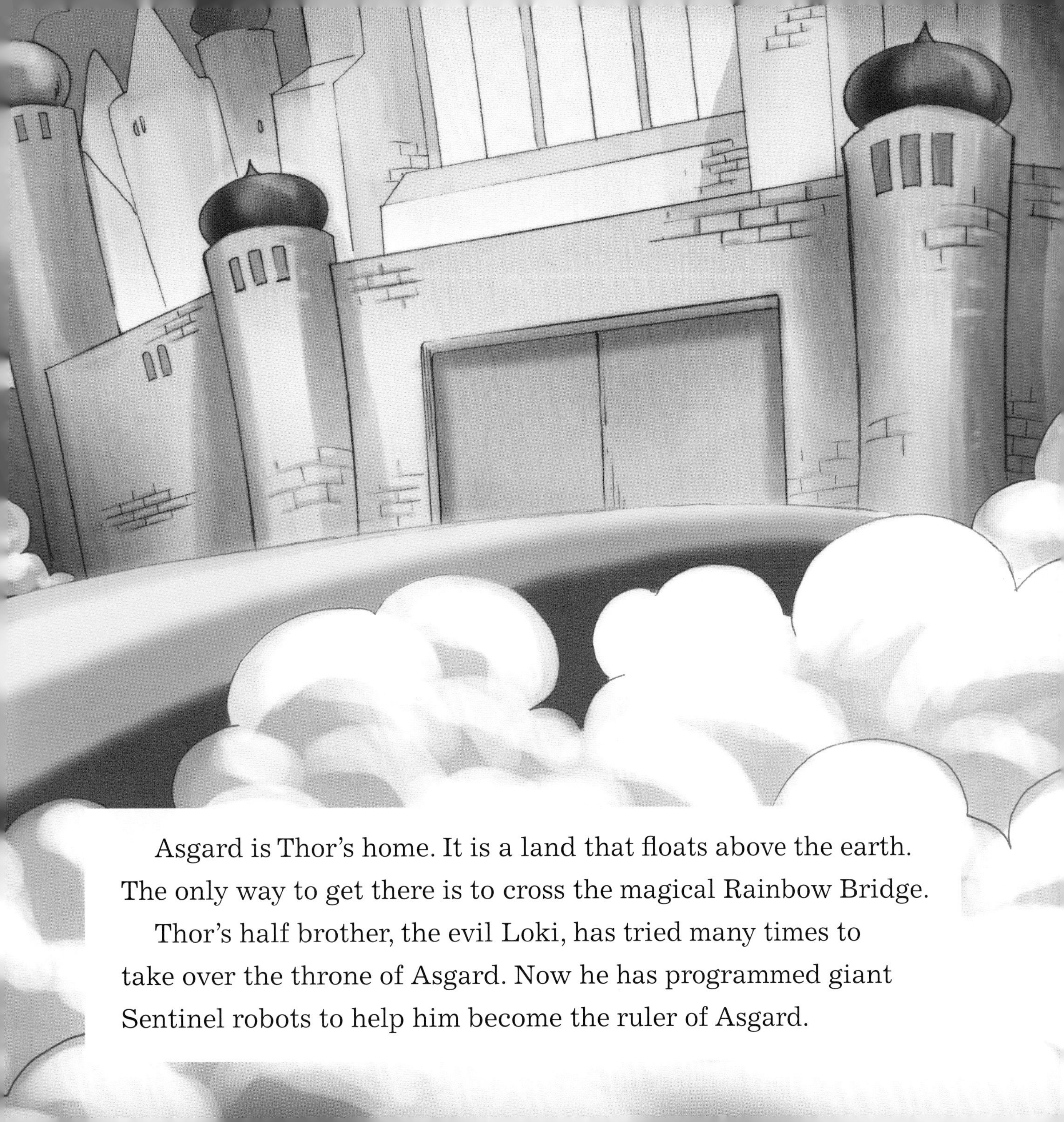

Asgard is Thor's home. It is a land that floats above the earth. The only way to get there is to cross the magical Rainbow Bridge.

Thor's half brother, the evil Loki, has tried many times to take over the throne of Asgard. Now he has programmed giant Sentinel robots to help him become the ruler of Asgard.

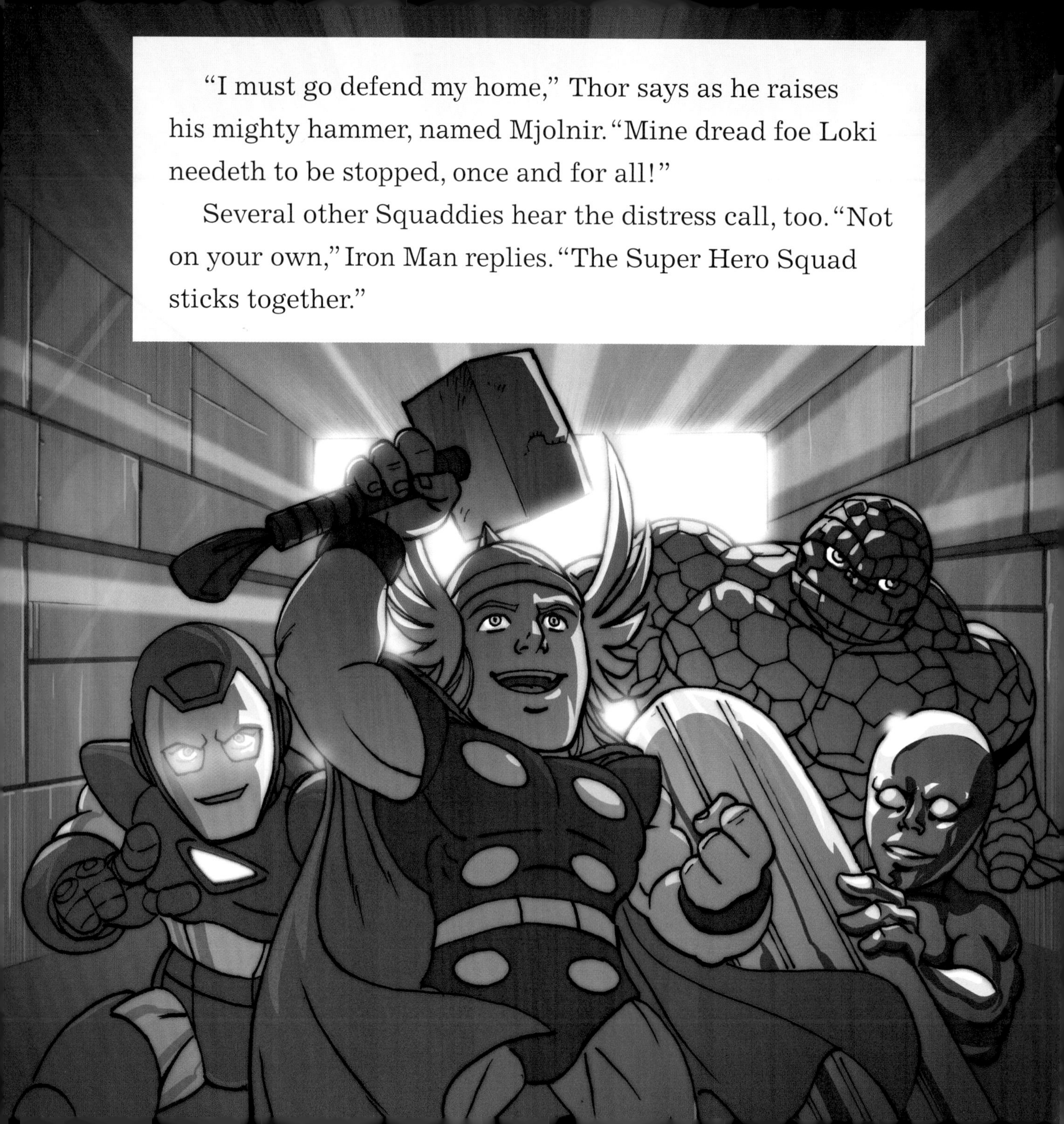

"I must go defend my home," Thor says as he raises his mighty hammer, named Mjolnir. "Mine dread foe Loki needeth to be stopped, once and for all!"

Several other Squaddies hear the distress call, too. "Not on your own," Iron Man replies. "The Super Hero Squad sticks together."

"We got your back," the Human Torch says as the Super Hero Squad races to Asgard. The Silver Surfer and the Thing are along for the ride, too.

From Asgard, Loki sees the Squad approaching. "So, my half brother and his Super Hero dudes think they can stop me?" Loki says with a laugh. "Soon the powers of Asgard will be mine!" He signals the Sentinels to attack.

“Me thinketh thou spoke too soon, brother!” Thor calls as he swings his hammer at the oncoming giants.

“Out of my way, beach bum,” the Thing yells as he pushes past the Silver Surfer. “I gots Sentinels to deal with.”

Working as a team, the Super Hero Squad drives Loki and the Sentinels back toward the Rainbow Bridge.
The Thing uses his rocky shoulders to bust through the robots like a bowling ball knocking down pins.
"Strike!" he shouts.

Just then one of the Sentinels shoots a blast of ice-cold energy at the Thing. The hero instantly freezes into an unbreakable block of ice. Three Sentinels scoop up the frozen Thing and carry him off.

Without the indestructible Thing to stop them, the robot army pushes past the Super Hero Squad. Using powerful blasts of energy, the Sentinels batter the gates of Asgard. Some of them shoot out cables that attach to the walls. Then the robots begin to yank down pieces of stone.

Thor hatches a plan. "Surfer, you and the Human Torch goeth forth to rescue the Thing," Thor orders. "We will hold off Loki until you return."

"You got it, Thor," the Silver Surfer replies. He and the Human Torch fly off after the Sentinels.

Thor zaps Loki with lightning strikes from his hammer, but Loki uses his magical abilities to conjure a shield.

The Sentinels surround Iron Man. His repulsor blasts keep them back, but there are too many robots for him to defeat alone. The Super Hero Squad is in trouble!

The Silver Surfer and the Human Torch catch up to the three robots who took their friend.

One of the Sentinels sees them and lifts a huge boulder. He hurls it at the two heroes. The Surfer shoots a cosmic blast at the rock, smashing it into a million pebbles. The giants toss more huge rocks at the hero, but he dodges each one as he surfs through the air.

While the Surfer keeps the Sentinels busy, the Human Torch blasts a stream of fire at the frozen Thing. The ice begins to melt, and the Thing smashes out of his icy prison.

"Freedom!" the Thing yells. The three giant robots turn and run off.

Back at the gates of Asgard, the heroes are losing the battle. The Sentinels smash through to the fortress.

"Time to surrender, brother," Loki yells. "Your forces are spread too thin. Asgard will fall soon, and I will finally take my place as its new ruler . . . the Mighty Loki, king of Asgard!"

Just then the Thing, the Silver Surfer, and the Human Torch return to the battle. Thor and Iron Man cheer.

"Time to Hero Up, Squaddies," Iron Man calls out as he leads a new charge against the Sentinels.

One of the Sentinels tries again to freeze the Thing, but the Silver Surfer deflects the blast with a burst of cosmic energy. The giant's icy stream goes off at an angle—right into his fellow robots! Several Sentinels are frozen in their tracks.

The Thing swings another Sentinel around by the arm and flings him toward the others, who are trading ice and fire with the Human Torch. The Sentinels collide as Iron Man uses his energy repulsors to knock them back through the gates of Asgard and off the Rainbow Bridge.

"And he picks up the spare!" shouts the Thing.

Loki stands alone, surrounded by the Super Hero Squad. Thor grabs his half brother by the shirt and lifts him off the ground.

"Looketh like thou hast failed again, my brother," Thor says with a smile.

Asgard is safe! Thor and the Super Hero Squad stand in the throne room with the Asgardian who called for help.

"Verily I say upon thee, Super Hero Squad, a job well done," he says. "Thank you."

Thor looks at his hero friends and smiles. "Well done, indeed!"